T0381206

Wally Wuzzlemoore Meets Little Miss Hate-It

Written and Illustrated by
Tom Schinderling

AuthorHouse™
1663 Liberty Drive
Bloomington, IN 47403
www.authorhouse.com
Phone: 1 (800) 839-8640

Published by AuthorHouse 09/03/2015

ISBN: 978-1-5049-3420-6 (sc)
ISBN: 978-1-5049-3421-3 (e)

Library of Congress Control Number: 2015914154

Print information available on the last page.

Wally jumped out of bed, happy as can be.

He rushed to eat his breakfast to fill his tummy.

He packed his backpack with everything he would need,

Preparing himself for an exciting deed.

Molly, his mother, was happy to see him full of joy.

She loved to see that Wally was an eager little boy.

Wally thought this new adventure was super cool,

For today was Wally's first day of school.

Wally strolled to the bus stop while Molly waved good-bye.

He felt a rush of good feelings as Molly tried not to cry.

She was proud to see him go with so much gusto

That it made her eyes tear up with joy and overflow.

3

Wally hopped on the bus and greeted its driver.
He saw his friend Jinx and gave him a high-fiver.
On the bus were also his friends Feathers and Globbity Glook.
They were showing each other their favorite book.

The bus ride was not long but just long enough.
He enjoyed the ride through town, seeing new kinds of stuff.
Wally had never traveled this far across town from his home;
The park across the street was as far as he could roam.

After the bus arrived at the school, Wally got a chill.

He could not wait to see; this would be quite the thrill.

He looked at the school in awe as he stood on the grass,

Wondering what would be taught in his first class.

Suddenly Wally heard some loud commotion from afar.

Someone was coming. Then he heard a loud *"Rawr!"*

Little monsters ran fleeing this way and that way

As one monster girl tormented others, thinking it was okay.

That is not okay, thought Wally as he oversaw.
The girl punched one kid and threatened another with her claw.
"Stay far away from her," said Wally's friend Jinx.
"She is the only thing about this school that stinks."

"That girl," explained Feathers, "is Little Miss Hate-It.
She will find out what you like and berate it.
No one knows why she is like this.
She is just one mean little miss."

Wally watched as the girl slapped another kid,

As Globbity Glook shared what else he knew she did.

"She will step on your toes to hear you cry.

She does not tell the truth; she prefers to lie."

Wally asked, "Does she not have a friend?"

"Wally," Jinx answered, "that would be a monster's end!

She says, 'Hey loser!' instead of hello.

She is quite uptight and never mellow."

11

Wally's joy for school began to change to fear;

This may end up being a long, scary year.

"She will throw dirt in your face and call you a name."

Added Feathers, "Then she will say that you are to blame!"

All these things scared Wally until Jinx said this:

"But there is one thing to be happy about Little Miss.

She is a grade older than us and not in our class,

And of course, having all four of us together will be a blast!"

Wally's expression of fear changed back to one of glee.
They all walked to their classroom to see what they could see.
Wally loved his new classroom and found a desk with his name.
The boys joked and giggled at their desks until the teacher came.

"Hello, class," she said sweetly. "I am Ms. Greenglove,
And I will be your teacher because teaching is what I love."
Wally smiled and was happy to have such a kind teacher.
She had four bright-blue eyes and was a beautiful creature.

"First we will start with how to ask for the hall pass—"
A sudden knock at the door interrupted Ms. Greenglove's class.
Standing there next to the principal, Mr. Mudslide,
Stood the unpleasant-looking monster girl from outside.

THE GOLDEN
RULE

TREAT OTHER
MONSTERS
THE WAY
YOU WOULD
LIKE TO BE
TREATED

Mr. Mudslide spoke quietly to Ms. Greenglove and then left,

Leaving behind Little Miss Hate-It and all her heft.

"It looks like I get the joy of having you another year,"

Said Ms. Greenglove to Little Miss. "Now take a seat, dear."

She walked over and took the empty seat behind Wally.

This put him in shock, and he no longer felt jolly.

Why was she in his class and not another?

Wally now wished he was back home with his mother.

The teacher went on to teach a lesson, then two.

Wally tried to learn all he could that was new.

And his handwriting on his paper would have been neat,

If not for being bumped by Little Miss kicking his seat.

Her feet would kick, kick, and kick some more.

This began to make Wally's fuzzy little bottom sore.

He politely raised his hand and told Ms. Greenglove.

Little Miss Hate-It stopped kicking, before giving Wally a shove.

Ms. Greenglove scolded little Miss Hate-It, but that was all.
She sat quietly until Ms. Greenglove stepped out into the hall.
Then Little Miss Hate-It got up and stood next to Wally's chair.
"You are really small, like a baby. Are you made of baby hair?"

She spoke cruelly toward him, teasing him about his size.
Wally did not know what to do as tears filled his eyes.
Little Miss took her seat when the teacher made her return.
Wally now felt sick, as his stomach began to turn.

The class was dismissed to go to recess break.

At last some fresh air, thought Wally, *for goodness' sake!*

He tried to go play on the swings, but

Little Miss was already there,

He wanted to stay clear of her; to swing he did not dare.

He climbed to the top of the slide and looked down,

But what he saw standing at the bottom made him frown.

There was Little Miss Hate-It shouting at him,

Making fun of his one little noodle-limb.

When he finally slid down, she pushed him into the sand.

He hurt his knee and did not want to stand.

She stood over him and called him names until the bell rang,

She skipped back inside, a cruel song she sang ...

"Wally is a bawly ball of baby hair.

He has a tiny head that's full of hot air!

He has only one limb, it is so dumb.

Wally is a bawly, little baby bum!"

Wally could not focus the rest of the school day.

He did not know what to do or to say.

Little Miss Hate-It picked on him until he got on the bus.

He tried not to cry on the way home or make a fuss.

31

He walked into his home with his head hung low.

Molly asked him, "Wally, how did your day go?"

Wally could not hold back his feelings any longer and let it out.

He bawled, declaring today was his worst

day ever, without a doubt!

Molly took him into her arms and asked him, "Why?"

Wally told her about his day as he had a good cry.

She held him close and let him get it all out.

She waited until the tears were gone and he was dry as a drought.

"Wally, my son," Molly said, "you have a bully at school.
But you can stand up to that bully and tell her you are no fool."
"But Mommy," Wally pleaded, "I am too little to stand up to her.
She is so big, and she tells other kids I wear a diaper."

"I was one of the littlest monsters, just like you,"
Molly told Wally, "and I had a bully too."
"What did you do, Mommy?" asked Wally of his mother.
"I stood up to him," she said, "and then he was no bother."

"You just tell her to stop it and that you are not her fool,"
Molly said, "and that she does not rule that school."
Wally smiled. "Do you think she will then leave me alone?"
"Yes," said Molly happily. "Just make your feelings known."

35

The next day of school started out just like the first.
Wally was ready to forget about the day he thought was his worst.
He was prepared to stand up against Little Miss Hate-It.
She would no longer pick on his size and berate it.

Wally saw Little Miss on the grass headed right toward him.
The other monsters thought this showdown was looking grim.
She stood over Wally, towering over his small size.
She glared down at him while he stared back into her eyes.

She opened her mouth to say something cruel to him.

"Stop it!" yelled Wally. "I know I have one little limb!"

Little Miss Hate-It's eyes were big in shock.

"And I know I am small," continued Wally, "but I rock!"

"No one else is like me, and that makes me cool!

And I am here to let you know I am not your fool!"

Wally laughed and hopped around while others kids joined in

While Little Miss Hate-It could not believe what had happened.

39

The rest of Wally's school day went by great;

No more bullying was heard of and no more hate.

Little Miss Hate-It became silent and never spoke a word.

She did not bully a single jock, goth, or nerd.

The next day after school, Wally could hear kids shout;

He decided to go over and check the noise out.

There was a group of kids standing in a ring.

They were around Little Miss Hate-It and began to sing ...

"This is Little Miss Hate-It.

She will find out what you like and berate it!

No one knows why she is like this.

She is just one mean little miss!"

43

44

Wally saw the tears in Little Miss's eyes fill full.

All of the kids teasing her made Wally feel awful.

Wally's feelings built up so much he had a fit.

At the top of his lungs he yelled, "Stop it!

"No one is like her," Wally said, "and I think that's cool!

And I am here to let you know she is not your fool!"

All the kids stood quiet looking at Wally.

His upset words made them feel their folly.

The children left feeling bad for what they did.

Little Miss Hate-It's hands still kept her face hid.

Wally reached out his palm and said, "Everything is all right."

Little Miss Hate-It thought Wally was a beautiful sight.

"Come along with me, Little Miss Hate-It," said Wally.

"That's not my name," she said. "It is Little Miss Holly."

Wally smiled at Holly. "I like that much better."

And he told Holly he was glad to have met her.

Little Miss Holly smiled big and started to laugh.

Wally shared a joke about a nosey giraffe.

He held her hand as they walked away;

This may have to be Wally's best day.

About the Author

Tom Schinderling received a BA in fine arts with a double specialization in fine art and multigraphic design from Northern State University. He uses a wide variety of media to tell fantastical stories, from paintings and sculptures to short films and animations. He currently resides in Aberdeen, South Dakota, and continues to find ways to share his unique imagination with others.

Printed in the United States
By Bookmasters